little Miss Quick

by Roger Hargreaves

Little Miss Quick was always in a terrible hurry and she was always trying to get everything done as quickly as she could.

Now, all this rushing around meant that Little Miss Quick was very careless.

She made her bed so quickly that it was in more of a mess afterwards than when she started!

When she brushed her teeth she squeezed
the toothpaste out of the tube so quickly
that it went everywhere.

Everywhere, that is, except on her toothbrush.

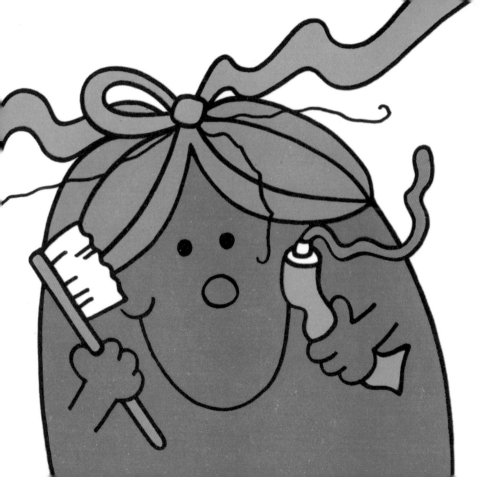

One sunny autumn morning,
Little Miss Quick got up even more quickly
than usual, and made her bed and combed
her hair in her quick and careless way.

After a breakfast of bread
(Little Miss Quick was always in far too
much of a hurry to wait for the toaster!)
she ran out of the house like a whirlwind,
and left the door open, as usual.

One minute later,
and three miles from her house,
Little Miss Quick came to a sudden stop.

The postman was standing in her way.

"You have far too many letters to deliver," she said.

"Let me help you."

And she delivered the letters very quickly.

But also very carelessly!

The postman was very angry.

In fact, he was so angry that he chased after Little Miss Quick...

...but she was already miles away.

She had met Mr Strong.

"That basket of eggs looks heavy," she said.

"Let me help you carry it back to your house."

And before Mr Strong had had a chance to say
'no', or even blink for that matter,
Little Miss Quick had carried the eggs back to
his house very quickly...

...and, needless to say, very carelessly!

When he saw that all his eggs were broken,
Mr Strong was furious.

In fact, he was so furious that he also
chased after Little Miss Quick.

But she was already miles away.

She was at the zoo
talking to the zoo keeper.

"You must be tired of
feeding all these lions,
let me feed them for you," she said.

Then before you could say 'Little Miss Quick',
she had picked up a bucket of corn and rushed off.

And fed the lions in her usual
quick...and very careless way.

Lions hate corn!

But they love doors
that are left open.

So it happened that,
on that sunny autumn morning,
Little Miss Quick found herself surrounded
by a very angry postman,
a furious Mr Strong,
a terrified zoo keeper,
and two hungry lions.

What do you think she did?

That's right!

Quick as a shot she said to herself,
"I'd better get out of here as quickly as
ever I can and...

...as carefully as possible!"

3 Great Offers for MR.MEN Fans!

MR. MEN TOKEN

1 New Mr. Men or Little Miss Library Bus Presentation Cases

A brand new stronger, roomier school bus library box, with sturdy carrying handle and stay-closed fasteners.

The full colour, wipe-clean boxes make a great home for your full collection.

They're just £5.99 inc P&P and free bookmark!

☐ MR. MEN ☐ LITTLE MISS (please tick and order overleaf)

2 Door Hangers and Posters

In every Mr. Men and Little Miss book like this one, you will find a special token. Collect 6 tokens and we will send you a brilliant Mr. Men or Little Miss poster and a Mr. Men or Little Miss double sided full colour bedroom door hanger of your choice. Simply tick your choice in the list and tape a 50p coin for your two items to this page.

PLEASE STICK YOUR 50P COIN HERE

Door Hangers (please tick)
☐ Mr. Nosey & Mr. Muddle
☐ Mr. Slow & Mr. Busy
☐ Mr. Messy & Mr. Quiet
☐ Mr. Perfect & Mr. Forgetful
☐ Little Miss Fun & Little Miss Late
☐ Little Miss Helpful & Little Miss Tidy
☐ Little Miss Busy & Little Miss Brainy
☐ Little Miss Star & Little Miss Fun

Posters (please tick)
☐ MR.MEN
☐ LITTLE MISS

3 Sixteen Beautiful Fridge Magnets – any 2 for £2.00! inc.P&P

They're very special collector's items!
Simply tick your first and second* choices from the list below
of any 2 characters!

1st Choice
- ☐ Mr. Happy
- ☐ Mr. Lazy
- ☐ Mr. Topsy-Turvy
- ☐ Mr. Bounce
- ☐ Mr. Bump
- ☐ Mr. Small
- ☐ Mr. Snow
- ☐ Mr. Wrong

- ☐ Mr. Daydream
- ☐ Mr. Tickle
- ☐ Mr. Greedy
- ☐ Mr. Funny
- ☐ Little Miss Giggles
- ☐ Little Miss Splendid
- ☐ Little Miss Naughty
- ☐ Little Miss Sunshine

2nd Choice
- ☐ Mr. Happy
- ☐ Mr. Lazy
- ☐ Mr. Topsy-Turvy
- ☐ Mr. Bounce
- ☐ Mr. Bump
- ☐ Mr. Small
- ☐ Mr. Snow
- ☐ Mr. Wrong

- ☐ Mr. Daydream
- ☐ Mr. Tickle
- ☐ Mr. Greedy
- ☐ Mr. Funny
- ☐ Little Miss Giggles
- ☐ Little Miss Splendid
- ☐ Little Miss Naughty
- ☐ Little Miss Sunshine

*Only in case your first choice is out of stock.

--- TO BE COMPLETED BY AN ADULT ---

**To apply for any of these great offers, ask an adult to complete the coupon below and send it with
the appropriate payment and tokens, if needed, to MR. MEN OFFERS, PO BOX 7, MANCHESTER M19 2HD**

☐ Please send ____ Mr. Men Library case(s) and/or ____ Little Miss Library case(s) at £5.99 each inc P&P

☐ Please send a poster and door hanger as selected overleaf. I enclose six tokens plus a 50p coin for P&P

☐ Please send me ____ pair(s) of Mr. Men/Little Miss fridge magnets, as selected above at £2.00 inc P&P

Fan's Name _____

Address _____

_____ **Postcode** _____

Date of Birth _____

Name of Parent/Guardian _____

Total amount enclosed £ _____

☐ **I enclose a cheque/postal order payable to Egmont Books Limited**

☐ **Please charge my MasterCard/Visa/Amex/Switch or Delta account** (delete as appropriate)

Card Number

Expiry date ___ / ___ **Signature** _____

Please allow 28 days for delivery. We reserve the right to change the terms of this offer at any time
but we offer a 14 day money back guarantee. This does not affect your statutory rights.

MR.MEN   LITTLE MISS
Mr. Men and Little Miss™ & ©Mrs. Roger Hargreaves

CUT ALONG DOTTED LINE AND RETURN THIS WHOLE PAGE